SUPER GRANDPA

David M. Schwartz
illustrated by **Bert Dodson**

return
to: Jack
slimm
814-68

TORTUGA PRESS
Santa Rosa, California

Sweden, 1951

For my Super Ma and my Super Pa

D.M.S.

For Gwyneth and Archer

B.D.

Inquiries should be addressed to: Tortuga Press, PMB: 181 2777 Yulupa Avenue, Santa Rosa, CA 95405 U.S.A. Tel. 707-544-4720

Library of Congress Cataloging-in-Publication Data
Schwartz, David M. Super Grandpa/ by David M. Schwartz; illustrated by Bert Dodson.   p. cm. Summary: A sixty-six-year-old grandfather, barred from entering the 1,000-mile Tour of Sweden because of his age, unofficially joins the bicycle race and, to the delight of his countrymen, emerges victorious.
ISBN 13: 978-1-889910-33-8 (hc)   ISBN 13: 978-1-889910-34-5 (pb)
ISBN 10: 1-889910-33-3 (hc)   ISBN 10: 1-889910-34-1 (pb)
[1. Grandfathers—Fiction. 2. Bicycle racing—Fiction. 3. Sweden—Fiction.]
1. Dodson. Bert. ill. II. Title III. Title: Super Grandpa. PZ7.S4073Su   2005 [E]—dc22
Library of Congress Control Number: 2004112935
2 3 4 5 6 7 8 9 10

Gustaf Håkansson was sixty-six years old. His hair was snow white, his beard a great white bush. His face rippled with wrinkles whenever he smiled. Gustaf Håkansson looked like an old man. But he didn't feel old, and he certainly didn't act old.

Everyone for miles around knew Gustaf. People saw him on his bicycle, rain or shine, riding through the crooked streets of Grantofta—past the baker's, the butcher's, and the wooden-toy maker's. Each morning, he pedaled over the stone bridge leading out of town, up steep hills scattered with farms, down narrow lanes bordered by stones, then home again to his morning paper and a bowl of yogurt and lingonberries.

One morning, Gustaf read something very exciting in the paper. There was going to be a bicycle race called the Tour of Sweden. It would be more than seventeen hundred kilometers—over one thousand miles—and it would last many days.

"This Tour of Sweden is for me!" exclaimed Gustaf.
"But you're too old for a bicycle race," said Gustaf's wife.
"You'd keel over," said his son. "It would be the end of you."

Even his grandchildren laughed at the idea. "You can't ride your bike seventeen hundred kilometers, Grandpa."

"*Struntprat!*" answered Gustaf. "Silly talk!" And he hopped onto his bike and rode off to see the judges of the race. He would tell them that he planned to enter the Tour of Sweden.

"But this race is for young people," the first judge explained.

"You're too old, Gustaf," scoffed the second judge. "You'd never make it to the finish."

"We can only admit racers who are strong and fit," insisted the third judge. "What if you collapsed in the middle of the race?"

"*Struntprat!*" protested Gustaf. "I have no intention of collapsing because I *am* strong and fit."

But the judges were not moved.

"We're sorry, Gustaf," one of them grumbled. "Go home. Go home to your rocking chair."

Gustaf went home, but he did not go to his rocking chair. "They can keep me out of the race," he muttered, "but they cannot keep me off the road."

The next morning, Gustaf began to prepare for the long race ahead. He arose with the sun, packed some fruit and rye bread, and cycled far out of town—over rolling hills dotted with ancient castles, across valleys dimpled with lakes, through forests thick with birches and pines. It was midafternoon before he returned. The next day he biked even farther. Each day he added more miles to his ride.

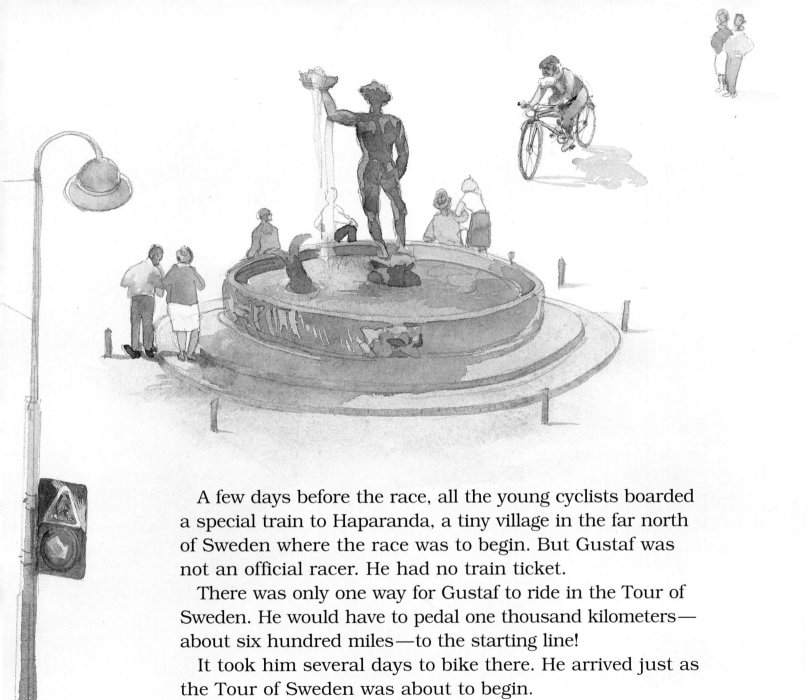

A few days before the race, all the young cyclists boarded a special train to Haparanda, a tiny village in the far north of Sweden where the race was to begin. But Gustaf was not an official racer. He had no train ticket.

There was only one way for Gustaf to ride in the Tour of Sweden. He would have to pedal one thousand kilometers—about six hundred miles—to the starting line!

It took him several days to bike there. He arrived just as the Tour of Sweden was about to begin.

All the racers wore numbers, but of course there was no number for Gustaf. So he found a scrap of bright red fabric and made his own.

What number should he be? He had an idea. He wasn't supposed to be in the race at all, so he would be Number Zero!

He chuckled as he cut out a big red zero and pinned it to his shirt. Then he wheeled his bicycle to the starting line.

The starting gun popped, and the young cyclists took off in a spurt. Their legs pumped furiously, and their bikes sprinted ahead. They soon left Gustaf far behind.

That night, the racers stopped at an inn. They were treated to dinner and a bed.

Hours later, Gustaf reached the inn. But there was no bed for him, so he just kept riding. While the others snoozed the night away, Gustaf pedaled into the dawn.

Early the next day, the other cyclists passed Gustaf. But he kept up his steady pace, and late that evening he again overtook the young racers as they rested. In the middle of the night, he napped for three hours on a park bench.

On the third morning, Gustaf was the first to arrive in the little town of Luleå. A small crowd of people waited, hoping to catch a glimpse of the racers zooming by. Instead they saw Gustaf. His white beard fluttered in the breeze. His red cheeks puffed with breath.

"Look!" cried a little girl. "Look! Here comes Super Grandpa!"

"Super Grandpa?" Everyone craned to see.

"Yes, yes! He does look like a super grandpa!"

A few clapped. Others shouted friendly greetings. Some of the children held out their hands and Gustaf brushed their palms as he rode by.

"Good luck to you, Super Grandpa!"

A photographer snapped Gustaf's picture. It appeared the next day in the newspaper. The headline read:

SUPER GRANDPA TAKES A RIDE.

Now all of Sweden knew about Super Grandpa Gustaf
Håkansson.

When he got hungry or thirsty, people gave him yogurt
with lingonberries, tea and cake, fruit juice, rye bread, or
any other snack he wanted.

Newspaper reporters rushed up to talk to him. Radio
interviewers broadcast every word he spoke. Everyone
wanted to know how he felt.

"I have never felt better in my whole life," he told them.

"But aren't you tired?" they asked.

"How can I be tired when I am surrounded by so much kindness?"

And with a push on the pedal and a wave of his hand, Gustaf was rolling down the road.

Once again, Gustaf rode through the night, passing the other racers as they slept. When his muscles felt stiff, he remembered his cheering fans. He pedaled harder.

And so it went, day after night, night after day. By the light of the moon, Gustaf quietly passed the young racers in their beds.

Then he slept outside, but only for a few hours. Under the long rays of the morning sun, they overtook him and left him behind, struggling to keep up his spirits and his pace. But each day it took them a little bit longer to catch up with Gustaf.

On the sixth morning of the race, thousands of people lined the road. As Gustaf rode by, their joyful cheers traveled with him like a wave through the crowd. He rode faster.

"You're almost there, Super Grandpa! Just a few more kilometers!"

"Don't look back. You're going to win!"

Win?

Gustaf hadn't thought about winning. He had simply wanted to ride in the Tour of Sweden and reach the finish line. But win?

"You're out in front, Super Grandpa!"

"A few more kilometers, and you'll be the winner!"

The winner? Gustaf glanced over his shoulder. The pack
of racers streaked across the last bridge. They hunched
their shoulders low over their handlebars. They raised
their backs high above their seats.

Gustaf decided not to think about them. Instead he
thought about his many fans. He thought about how they
wanted him to win. And suddenly he wanted to win too!

He looked ahead. In the distance he could see a bright blue banner stretched across the road. The finish line!

Gustaf lowered his head. He raised his back. He whipped his legs around with all their might and all their motion.

The next time he looked up, he was bursting through the banner and rolling over the finish line—just before the next racer thundered past.

The crowd roared. People lifted Gustaf onto their shoulders. They showered him with flowers. They sang victory songs. The police band played patriotic marches.

But the celebration did not make the three judges happy. They were furious. They said that Gustaf could not be the winner because he was never actually in the race. Besides, it was against the rules to ride at night. No, the big gold trophy would go to the next racer, not to Gustaf.

But no one seemed to care what the judges said. Even the king stepped up to hug Gustaf and invite him to the palace. And to nearly everyone in Sweden, the winner was Gustaf Håkansson—sixty-six years old, his hair as white as snow, his beard a great white bush, his smiling face an orb of wrinkles. To them, the winner of the Tour of Sweden was the man they all called Super Grandpa.

END
Fin.

A NOTE FROM THE AUTHOR

There really was a sixty-six-year-old Gustaf Håkansson who, in 1951, defied the judges and rode 1,761 kilometers (1,094 miles) in the *Sverige-Loppet* or "Tour of Sweden." It was the longest bicycle race that had ever been held in the history of Sweden.

A little girl who saw Gustaf on his bike awarded him the name *Stålfarfar*, which the rest of the nation quickly adopted. Literally, it means "Steel Grandfather," but Swedish children use the term *Stålman* for "Superman," so we have translated *Stålfarfar* as "Super Grandpa."

Cycling day and night, Gustaf did indeed finish first. In reality, he rode his own private race, starting several days before the other racers and finishing a full day ahead of the next competitor. In this telling, I changed some facts and added drama by creating a "tortoise and hare" story with a suspenseful finish. But in 1951, a sixty-six-year-old man bicycling more than 1,000 miles was dramatic enough. His feat captured the imagination and adoration of his countrymen, including the king. Gustaf Håkansson became a national hero.

After the race, admirers wrote to "Super Grandpa" from all over Sweden. Not knowing his address or his real name, many just wrote *Stålfarfar* on the envelope—and the post office knew where to deliver all the letters! Some people sent Gustaf expensive gifts, such as rocking chairs and mattresses so that he could take a well-deserved rest. Of all the things that came in the mail, Gustaf said his favorite was a letter that began, "I am your age, dear Gustaf Håkansson, and I was an ailing old man before you came along. But your example made me feel young, healthy and happy again. God bless you!"

The tale of Gustaf Håkansson's 1,000-mile bike ride lives on in Sweden, where *Stålfarfar* still enjoys the status of a folk hero. Parents encouraging their children to eat well, get plenty of exercise, and to try hard at whatever they do, tell them, "*Va' som Stålfarfar*," or "Be like Super Grandpa." In fact, Gustaf lived to be 102 and was still participating in bicycle races at the age of 85!

I wrote this book to spread the story of an ordinary man who performed in an extraordinary way. Few of Håkansson's Swedish fans wished to ride a bicycle 1,000 miles, but most—like people everywhere—harbored some sort of dream. The white-bearded cyclist blew life into his dream and showed that with enough drive and persistence, anyone can make a dream come true.

What's more, Super Grandpa shattered a stereotype. He suffered when society deemed senior citizens unfit, just as ethnic minorities, women, and those who are physically disabled suffer when society deems a whole class of people inferior or incompetent. Snubbed because of his age, Gustaf wasn't even allowed to try. But by defying the judges, he changed the way people think and, with his triumph, scored a victory for us all.

—D.M.S.